# Sam's Spots

First published in 2008 by
Franklin Watts
338 Euston Road
London
NW1 3BH

Franklin Watts Australia
Level 17/207 Kent Street
Sydney
NSW 2000

Text © Caryn Jenner 2008
Illustration © Jonathan Langley 2008

A CIP catalogue record for this book is available
from the British Library.

ISBN 978 0 7496 7976 7 (hbk)
ISBN 978 0 7496 7984 2 (pbk)

**Series Editor:** Jackie Hamley
**Series Advisor:** Dr Barrie Wade
**Series Designer:** Peter Scoulding

Printed in China

Franklin Watts is a division of
Hachette Children's Books,
an Hachette Livre UK company.

To Lia, with love – C.J.

# Sam's Spots

by Caryn Jenner

Illustrated by Jonathan Langley

## W
## FRANKLIN WATTS
LONDON•SYDNEY

# Sam was excited about his birthday.

He had invited lots of friends to his party.

7

But there was a problem.

Sam felt itchy all over.

"You're very spotty,"
said Dad the next day.

"You've got chicken pox,"
said Mum.

"We can't have your party until you're better," said Dad.

Sam was upset.

Mum gave Sam a bath
with special oil in it.

Dad covered Sam's spots
with special lotion.

His sister, Lily, tried
to cheer him up.

"Birthdays are full of surprises!" she said.

"Even spotty birthdays?"
Sam grumbled.

"Wait and see," smiled Lily.

On his birthday, Sam
woke up feeling sad.
Then Lily came into
his bedroom.

She had painted spots
all over her face.
Sam laughed.

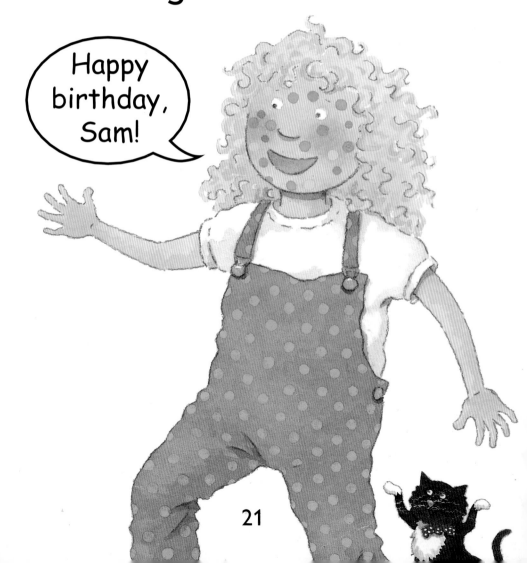

Happy
birthday,
Sam!

21

He laughed at Mum
and Dad, too.

"Now we're all spotty,"
said Mum.

There were lots of spotty surprises.

They all played pin the
spots on the donkey ...

... and pass the spotty parcel.

Then they ate spotty
birthday cake.

"There's one more spotty surprise," Lily told Sam.

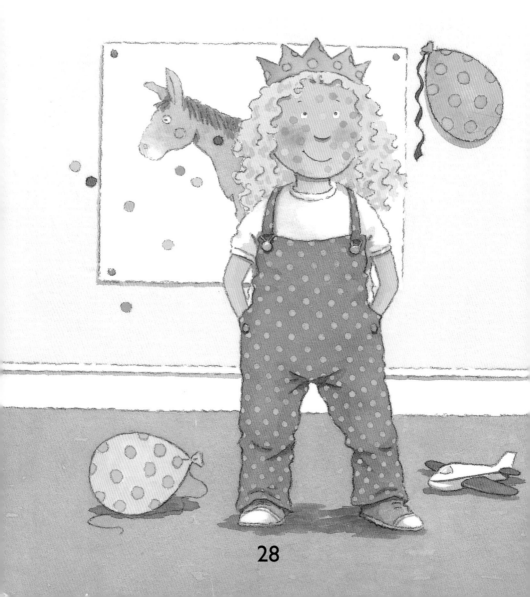

28

"Something you've always wanted."

"Spotty birthdays are the best! I'm going to call him Spot!" laughed Sam.

31

Leapfrog has been specially designed to fit the requirements of the National Literacy Framework. It offers real books for beginning readers by top authors and illustrators. There are 26 Leapfrog stories to choose from:

**The Bossy Cockerel**
ISBN 978 0 7496 3828 3

**Bill's Baggy Trousers**
ISBN 978 0 7496 3829 0

**Little Joe's Big Race**
ISBN 978 0 7496 3832 0

**The Little Star**
ISBN 978 0 7496 3833 7

**The Cheeky Monkey**
ISBN 978 0 7496 3830 6

**Selfish Sophie**
ISBN 978 0 7496 4385 0

**Recycled!**
ISBN 978 0 7496 4388 1

**Felix on the Move**
ISBN 978 0 7496 4387 4

**Pippa and Poppa**
ISBN 978 0 7496 4386 7

**Jack's Party**
ISBN 978 0 7496 4389 8

**The Best Snowman**
ISBN 978 0 7496 4390 4

**Mary and the Fairy**
ISBN 978 0 7496 4633 2

**The Crying Princess**
ISBN 978 0 7496 4632 5

**Jasper and Jess**
ISBN 978 0 7496 4081 1

**The Lazy Scarecrow**
ISBN 978 0 7496 4082 8

**The Naughty Puppy**
ISBN 978 0 7496 4383 6

**Big Bad Blob**
ISBN 978 0 7496 7092 4*
ISBN 978 0 7496 7796 1

**Cara's Breakfast**
ISBN 978 0 7496 7093 1*
ISBN 978 0 7496 7797 8

**Why Not?**
ISBN 978 0 7496 7094 8*
ISBN 978 0 7496 7798 5

**Croc's Tooth**
ISBN 978 0 7496 7095 5*
ISBN 978 0 7496 7799 2

**The Magic Word**
ISBN 978 0 7496 7096 2*
ISBN 978 0 7496 7800 5

**Tim's Tent**
ISBN 978 0 7496 7097 9*
ISBN 978 0 7496 7801 2

**Sticky Vickie**
ISBN 978 0 7496 7978 1*
ISBN 978 0 7496 7986 6

**Handyman Doug**
ISBN 978 0 7496 7979 8*
ISBN 978 0 7496 7987 3

**Billy and the Wizard**
ISBN 978 0 7496 7977 4*
ISBN 978 0 7496 7985 9

**Sam's Spots**
ISBN 978 0 7496 7976 7*
ISBN 978 0 7496 7984 2

## Look out for Leapfrog
## FAIRY TALES

**Cinderella**
ISBN 978 0 7496 4228 0

**The Three Little Pigs**
ISBN 978 0 7496 4227 3

**Jack and the Beanstalk**
ISBN 978 0 7496 4229 7

**The Three Billy Goats Gruff**
ISBN 978 0 7496 4226 6

**Goldilocks and the Three Bears**
ISBN 978 0 7496 4225 9

**Little Red Riding Hood**
ISBN 978 0 7496 4224 2

**Rapunzel**
ISBN 978 0 7496 6159 5

**Snow White**
ISBN 978 0 7496 6161 8

**The Emperor's New Clothes**
ISBN 978 0 7496 6163 2

**The Pied Piper of Hamelin**
ISBN 978 0 7496 6164 9

**Hansel and Gretel**
ISBN 978 0 7496 6162 5

**The Sleeping Beauty**
ISBN 978 0 7496 6160 1

**Rumpelstiltskin**
ISBN 978 0 7496 6165 6

**The Ugly Duckling**
ISBN 978 0 7496 6166 3

**Puss in Boots**
ISBN 978 0 7496 6167 0

**The Frog Prince**
ISBN 978 0 7496 6168 7

**The Princess and the Pea**
ISBN 978 0 7496 6169 4

**Dick Whittington**
ISBN 978 0 7496 6170 0

**The Elves and the Shoemaker**
ISBN 978 0 7496 6581 4

**The Little Match Girl**
ISBN 978 0 7496 6582 1

**The Little Mermaid**
ISBN 978 0 7496 6583 8

**The Little Red Hen**
ISBN 978 0 7496 6585 2

**The Nightingale**
ISBN 978 0 7496 6586 9

**Thumbelina**
ISBN 978 0 7496 6587 6

**Rhyming stories are available with Leapfrog Rhyme Time.**

* hardback